Florence and Her Fantastic Family Tree

To my grandchildren: Abby, Madalyn, Grace, Christian, and Radley.
—J.G.

To my lively nephew and niece, Luca and Beatrice.
—L.A.

Copyright © 2020 by Judy Gilliam
Illustration copyright © 2020 by Laura Addari
All rights reserved.

Published by Familius LLC, www.familius.com
1254 Commerce Way Sanger, CA 93657

Familius books are available at special discounts for bulk purchases, whether for
sales promotions or for family or corporate use. For more information,
contact Familius Sales at 559-876-2170 or email orders@familius.com.

Reproduction of this book in any manner, in whole or in part,
without written permission of the publisher is prohibited.

Library of Congress Control Number
2020936665

Print ISBN 9781641702508
Ebook ISBN 9781641703703

Printed in China

Edited by Kaylee Mason and Brooke Jorden
Cover and book design by Carlos Guerrero

10 9 8 7 6 5 4 3 2 1

First Edition

Florence
and Her
Fantastic
Family Tree

By
Judy Gilliam

Illustrations by
Laura Addari

At least Ms. Collin didn't assign
us a diorama for the family
project. She said, "Just create
a family tree." Like that was easy.

The problem is that my family tree doesn't just
have a trunk, roots, leaves, and branches. It has
stickers, thorns, and extra limbs. My family tree is
prickly, scaly, and partially overgrown.

My best friend Sonji's tree is
pretty simple—one mom, one dad, and one brother.
When she puts her family tree up on Ms. Collin's
classroom wall, it will look like this:

But mine will take three or four poster boards and
end up looking like a jungle of people.
You see, I don't have a neat little family.
I have extras.

There's me, Florence, and my brother, Fred. And we have four parents—well, make that six. You see my problem. How do I explain this?

Okay, first it was just my mom and dad—Betty and Bruce. They got married and had Fred and me.
TA-DA!

When Fred and I were really small, they broke up, and then Betty married James and Bruce married Lucy.

Are you counting?
That makes four parents now.

Betty and James ended up adopting Caitlin, my half-sister, and Bruce and Lucy came up with three of their own, my half-brothers Wills, Brian, and Percy.

Then, sadly, Bruce and Lucy divorced, and Bruce married Kate while Lucy married Fabian.

If you're still counting, that's six parents:
the original Betty and Bruce; Betty's
second husband, James; Bruce's second wife, Lucy;
followed by his third wife, Kate; and stepmother
Lucy's new husband, Fabian.
A total of six—hard to keep up, right?

As you can see, my family tree is going to take
up a lot of space on the classroom wall.

To add to the giant tree, Bruce and his wife, Kate, had a son, Sam, who is technically my half-brother.

That's a lot of kids.

There's me and Fred, then there is my half-sister, Caitlin, and the three half-brothers, Wills, Brian, and Percy.

Oh, and don't forget about new baby and half-brother, Sam. So, let's see what this family tree is going to look like now.

FRED

BRIAN

PERCY

CAITLIN

LITTLE
SAM

WILLS

Sometimes, even I get confused about all
my parents and siblings, so I worry that
my teacher and all the students
will be really confused too.

That's not my only worry—

Will my tree actually fit the space
on the wall?

What do I do if it's too big?

Can I explain who is who?
Will anyone believe me?

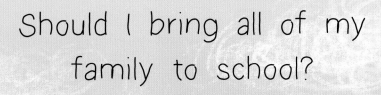

Should I bring all of my
family to school?

No, let's stick to paper.

I may need help taking it to class
and taping it to the wall, but here goes.

My family with all the parts—
stems, branches, leaves, trunk,
berries, and nuts.

It might *not* be simple and might *not* be easy to describe, but these are my people, and they're going to take up most of Ms. Collin's wall.

But you know what the best part is? That's me right in the middle of this great, big, loud, colorful, fun, crazy family that I call mine.

Next time, I'll include my grandparents—
must be twenty of them!